Anthology of:

My Poetry & I

BERT DIBISH

Trafford
PUBLISHING™

Order this book online at www.trafford.com/05-2150
or email orders@trafford.com

Most Trafford titles are also available at major online book retailers.

Printed in the United States of America.

ISBN: 978-1-4120-7255-7 (sc)

Trafford rev. 04/11/2011

   www.trafford.com

North America & international
toll-free: 1 888 232 4444 (USA & Canada)
phone: 250 383 6864 ♦ fax: 812 355 4082

Testimonials

Ever since I was a little girl, I have always liked to hear my dad read his poems, when you're sad he would write a poem to make me smile. He can write a poem for any occasion and for anything. His poems are from the bottom of his heart. They say a lot of things he can't say in person. There are so many words to describe the poems he writes, but the ones that stick out would be heartfelt and meaningful. When he writes they are beautiful. I haven't met anyone who didn't like the poems my dad writes. Everyone enjoys reading and hearing them. Everyone wants copies of these poems if they really enjoy them. My dads poems are very special and they are everything. He is bright, wonderful and enjoyable.

   B. WOOD

My name is Arby and I am writing in to tell you know how much I adore Berts poems he writes. I'm his girlfriend and the poems he writes tells his feelings. That is how he expresses himself, they are warm and very loving. If any man is having a problem getting his feelings out to his girlfriends, or wives, they should go to Bert's poems and pick out a poem and leave it with their wives or girlfriends. He can make you feel so special with these poems. I would call it a romantic swirl. Bert works really hard on these poems and he has a great talent for this. I'm glad he is finally getting a book published on these. They are too good to let sit around. Hope everyone enjoys them as much as I do. Remember when something good happens, God is up to something. And it has came true for him.

   ARBY

Bert's poetry is filled with honest emotion and sincerity. Each of his poems is a short glimpse into his soul. They chronicle his love, his heartbreak, his pain and his joys. Bert gives us a small window into his world and there is no room left to doubt that he is a man of great sensitivity. His works appeal to me because they illustrate how deeply each and every person that touches his life impact him along his journey.

⌐BECKY

Bert, your poems touch my heart and kiss my soul. You amaze me with your beautiful talent of expressing what I am feeling and not able to explain to myself. Thank you for sharing your soul with me. I love you.

⌐TAMMIE MARTINEZ

Bert,
Your poetry is an inspiration. I am grateful to have shared this time with you and been here throughout your journey. You have more than inspired me, you have moved me down to my soul. Don't stop the beautiful life lessons or peaks in your heart.

⌐HEATHER

I personally have always enjoyed his poetry. It has warm and enduring qualities that leave you with a smile in your heart making it very easy to say yes, I have felt that way too!

⌐VICKIE

Dedication

THESE DEDICATIONS ARE FOR THE FOLLOWING PEOPLE:

To my new girlfriend Arby, who really loves my poems and me. Thank you very much hun.

To my ex wife (Virginia Camp, Dibish, Mills) who actually got me started in writing my poetry. Cause she liked them and showed our friends who also liked them. Thank you.

My four daughters Donna, Sherry, Angel and Brenda, who also liked them. Thank you also.

And Becky H, Heather, Tammie M, Vickie M.

To my brother Bob Sr. and sister in law Peggy.

To my girls, my nephew Robert Jr. my neice in law Vicki, grand neice Allison, neice Sheila, and nephew John and neice Kayla.

I really love each and everyone of you, and thank you from the bottom of my heart.

Table of Contents

To A Very Special Person

TO RRF, WHO HELPED ME TREMENDOUSLY

You were sent to me, in my times of need,
We became friends, yes indeed.

You helped me, with my physical health,
As well as, my emotional, and mental health.

I was really ready, to give it all up,
But you came, and picked me back up.

With your kindness, and Godly thought,
A new life to me, you have brought.

I'll never forget, what you have, done for me,
Within my heart, you will always be.

You will always be, my special friend,
Always and forever, to the very end.

Because you are, a very special friend,
May God bless you, to the very end.

Amandas Nephew

TO LOWER SALEM, OH {LEBANON, OH}

Down here, Amandas Nephew, left this life,
But it'll save him, from a life of strife.
He was only, THREE WEEKS OLD,
Born without intestines, we've been told.
Can't get the right words, off our tongue,
To lose someone, so very young.
It's so sad, to have to let go,
To lose this, very little fellow.
But in this case, with this little guy,
He'll be happy with God, in heaven in the sky.
Some may call this, a bit of treason,
Remember, everything happens, for a reason.
Keep your faith, and continue to pray,
You'll get another chance, another day.
Our sympathy, and condolences, go out to you,
Our prayers, and love, are also with you.
With you, we will ride this tide,
We will always, be by your side.

Little Brittany

This whole town, had such a fright,
Brittany became missing, Tuesday night.
A lot of people were, out searching for her,
But they were, unable to find her.
She was a lovely, seven year old,
The sweetest girl, you'd ever want to hold.
She was found, the next day, deep in a well,
Who ever did this, should go straight to hell.
A little girl does not, deserve this fate,
If you need help, please call, don't hesitate.
We will stand by you, all the way,
We will help you survive, in any way.
Our sympathy and condolences, are with you,
Our prayers and love, are being sent too.
There's no monetary value, to cover the cost,
Of your sad, and very tragic loss.
We have sorrow, in our hearts for you.

Look To The Lord

When you feel, you really need help,
Should you stand there, and scream and yelp?
When you feel, there's nowhere to look,
Why not try looking, in the holy book.
LOOK TO THE LORD
When you feel lonely, and very sad,
Cause everything around you, has turned bad.
When you feel like, you're in total despair,
You and the Lord, can make a heavenly pair.
LOOK TO THE LORD
When you look for someone, for you to save,
You don't have to be, big and brave.
Heavenly things, will come to you,
If you know, just what to do.
LOOK TO THE LORD
He will save, and guide you,
This is all, you have to do.
LOOK TO THE LORD

Follow His Way

Now start, the two thousand five year,
I hope it isn't a year, of a lot of tears.
I hope it will all be, safe and sound,
With much happiness, that can be found.
We should be able, to live a happy life,
Without tears, tragedies, and of strife.
Let's all let all of, our love be released,
And try to live in, harmony and in peace.
We should be living, for one and another,
Not quarelling, and fighting, with each other.
We should take lessons, from God up above,
And get along, and share His true love.
God loves each one of us, one and all
No matter how big, or no matter how small.
We should listen, and follow in His ways,
And live and make these, our happy days.
Our life would be, much better this way,
If we would pull together, and try to pray.

Our Savior

If you need, a heavenly favor,
Why not look, up to our Savior?
If you want, a great hook up,
Our Lord will be there, to pick you up.
If you feel really, down in your life,
The Lord will give you, a brighter life.
Just ask Him, to please guide you,
And He surely, will see you thru.
He will give you, His special gift,
And give you, His spiritual lift.
Beg, borrow or steal, is not His accord,
He wants us to listen, to his word.
The end, in heaven, you want to be living?
His word down here, you should be living.
If reaching heaven, is your final goal,
Just ask Him to please, cleanse your soul.
He will gladly, show you the way,
To meet him, on your final day.
This is the way, of our Savior.

Stop, Praise, And Ask The Lord

Sometimes we sit, and wonder, and think,
And that almost brings, us to the brink.
We're about to do, something wrong,
Even though we know, it's totally wrong.

STOP AND PRAISE THE LORD

We can't help ourselves, feeling this way,
Something always happens, to us everyday.
We should get down, on our knees and pray,
Help and guide us, dear Lord, this very day.

AND GIVE PRAISE TO THE LORD

We know for Him, this is no great task,
All we have to do, is pray and ask.
He loves us with, His Holy Heart,
He will give us, a brand new start.

JUST STOP, AND ASK THE LORD

Now you know what, you should do,
For divine help, the rest is up to you.

STOP, PRAISE, AND ASK THE LORD

Yo Dawg

TO ALL YOU WHO THO'T YOU WERE SO COOL!!!

Yo Dawg, you raunchy mutt,
Struttin' with your, soulful strut.
With everyone, that you meet,
Think they have to, bow down at your feet.
You know you, ain't too bright,
Time to stand up, and fly right.
Cause you been, so awful bad,
You got a lot, of people really mad.
You done some things, you shouldn't oughtta,
Turn it around, and do right, you gotta.
Don't sit back, and try to act shy,
I know you can do it, if you try.
Listen son, don't try to be coy,
You're no longer, a little boy.
It's time to finally, take a stand,
Stand up and finally, be a man.
Yo Dawg, no longer be a mutt,
No longer "struttin'", that soulful strut.

Thumpin', Jumpin', Poundin' Heart

You gave me a Thumpin', Jumpin', Poundin Heart,
It damn near, blew itself apart.
You gave it, a quick jump start,
My Thumpin', Jumpin', Poundin Heart.
The way you passed by, and said HI,
I tho't my heart was, just gonna stop and die.
The way you walked, and shuffled your feet,
I knew you were a girl, I just had to meet.
The way you walked by, without a care,
Your long beautiful hair, flowing in the air.
I just had to make you, mine all mine,
Us always being together, for all time.
But, do you know what, you surely did?
You gave me a Thumpin' Jumpin' Poundin' Heart,
It damn near, blew itself apart.
You gave it a, quick jump start,
My Thumpin', Jumpin', Poundin' Heart.

Happy Mothers Day

Today is, Mothers Day.
It's supposed to be, your special day,
We all feel, it's supposed to be that way.
Somehow, somewhere, along the way,
We tend to forget, what we're to do today.
And what we're supposed, to feel this day,
Our hearts are with you, on this day.
But our actions, show you another way,
We do not mean, to be this way.
Taking you for granted, is just our way,
Of daily tasks, from us, day to day.
We know you will be there, for us everyday,
So we just forget, to show our love everyday.
DON'T EVER FORGET, we love you in every way,
We love you, unconditionally, everyday.
The most important thing, we want to say,
We love you Mom, "HAPPY MOTHERS DAY" !!!!

For Fathers Day

FOR OUR FATHERS, WHOM WE LOVE

Fathers Day, is here, for this week,
Cards and special gifts, we do seek.
We try to get something, better each year,
For our Dads, who are very dear.
When trouble arises, he never tries to hide,
You can always find him, by our side.
He tries to teach us, the right way to live,
Love, strength, understanding, he does give.
Sometimes our pride, we have to swallow,
Shows us which path, we should try to follow.
He tries to praise us, with a favorite song,
He tries to teach us, to never do wrong.
And all through life, never try to lie,
Always try to be righteous, until we die.
We are really happy, and very glad,
That this, particular man, is our Dad.
On a pedestal, is really, where he should be,
For everyone in, the entire world to see.

Our Joyous Season

It's now only, a couple weeks away,
Then it will be, Christmas Day.
Kids anticipate it, with all their joy,
Hoping to get all kinds, of gifts and toys.
Adults really like it, very much too,
Giving and receiving, a lot of gifts too.
It is really time, to deck the halls,
Christmas time is for all, big and small.
Singing Christmas Carols, and their rhymes,
Everyone will be having, a very good time,
But let's not forget, the Real Reason,
Why we really have, this Joyous Season.
Let's keep Christ, in our Christmas theme,
Let's put HIM where, he can be heard and seen
Let's not be afraid, to say we believe,
And for HIM, in our hearts, to receive.
"MERRY CHRISTMAS", TO ONE AND ALL,
AND A VERY GOOD NIGHT, TO YOU ALL.

It's Christmas Time

Once again, it's Christmas time,
With Christmas carols, and their rhymes.
Everybody loves, this time of year,
Cause Christmas, is finally here.
Time for, the Ill Winds, to blow,
Time for the, wonderous snow.
Kids love it, as they frolic and play,
All their worries, and cares go away.
As they slide, and ride their sleds,
Only having fun, is in their heads.
Rosy cheeks, and cherry noses,
They go uphill, for another dose.
Time to give gifts, and to receive,
The gifts we'll get, in which we believe.
But let's not forget, the "REAL REASON",
Why we have this, "GLORIOUS SEASON".

Thanksgiving

Why We Give Thanks!!
Once again, it's Thanksgiving,
Time to give thanks, cause we're still living.
Every morning, when we awake,
Be thankful, for every breath we take.
Look at the sun, as it rises in the sky,
The beautiful way it lights up the sky.
Be thankful for the grass, flowers and trees,
Being able to see, and enjoy all of these.
Thankful for the abundance, of food we eat
The fruit, cheese, veggies, and the meat.
Be thankful we don't, have to ask please,
We come and go, as we please.
Be thankful that, this is our "DECREE",
Cause we live in, the "THE LAND OF THE FREE"
We should not give thanks, one day a year,
We should give thanks all year, every year.
The Lord has given us, all "HIS LOVE".
He gave all of this, from Heaven above.
This is the reason, for our Thanksgiving.

Looking Towards Easter

A Very Special Holiday
Easter is, our next holiday,
Kids will be waiting, for that day.
Lots of good food, and tons of candy,
This will make them, feel, just dandy.
Families getting together, to be as one,
Kids will be outside, having fun.
We will all be, in a very festive mood,
Ham and Kolbasi, and all kinds of food.
Some potato salad, and deviled eggs too,
Some will even, have turkey too.
But no matter what, you cook, for your crew,
There'll be enough to feed you, thru and thru.
Kids wait for Easter Bunny, making his rounds,
To search for Easter eggs, he hid all around.
But no matter what, some people say,
This is a very, special, Glorious Day.
Do not forget why, we have this, Glorious Day.
God died on the cross, for us, on Good Friday,
Then rose again for us, on Easter Sunday.

Valentines Day

I'm sitting here thinking, of Valentines Day,
It is lovers, very special day.
Everybody showing, their loving feeling,
Making each others hearts, go a reeling.
Making sure, of our special love,
Thanking heaven, for sending your love.
I gave my heart, to only you,
No one else, will ever do.
My love for you, is felt thru and thru,
My heart belongs, to only you.
Writing this poem, is just one way,
To really show my love, on this special day.
Giving someone chocolates, and a card,
Isn't really very much, all that hard.
Sending true tho'ts, from your heart,
That's what will really, touch her heart.
But a poem like this, to your turtle dove,
Will show to her, your real true love.
That's what makes, a special Valentines Day.

Halloween Time

Once again it is, "Halloween Time",
For funny and scary, costume time.
Adults as well, as kids, looking for treats,
This time of the year, just can't be beat.
Kids will be running, around mighty hearty,
Adults will be having, their Halloween party.
Monsters, ghouls, and goblins and ghosts,
Witches and faries, will, visit their hosts.
To get all the goodies, that they can get,
Everyone is having their fun, you can bet.
Apples, candy, cookies, and even snack packs
Whatever they can carry, in their sacks.
From house to house, they search for treats,
And smile at the people, they each meet.
Not the costumes, and all their gear,
Wouldn't it be great, to be like this all year
Wouldn't it be great, to really go back,
As kids and carry, our little treat sacks?

Kid's Winter Thrill

Watch the kids, on yonder hill,
As they get, their winter thrill.
Slipping and sliding, down the hill,
With their voices, "Oh so shrill".
For them, the rest of the world, stands still,
As they get, their winter thrill.
Also, with snowball battles, to be won,
Oh, they are having, so much fun.
With noses and cheeks, so rosy red,
They continue, to slip, slide, and sled.
Not a care in the world, has anyone,
Because they are having, so much fun.
Oh, to be able to turn back, the hands of time,
As kids, to be back, in those wonderful times.
To be able to go back, on a similar hill,
Once again, getting, our winter thrill.

With every Breath,
That I Take

With every breath, that I take,
My whole body, does shake.
Just the tho't, of seeing you,
Makes my body, shake thru and thru.
You are definitely, one of a kind,
You are always, on my mind.
This is really, hard to believe,
But I can, hardly breathe.
You really take, my breath away,
That is why, I am this way.
My every tho't, is about you,
Don't know what, I'm gonna do.
You really got, my heart a reelin',
Don't exactly know, what I'm a feelin'.
I don't know if, there is a cure,
But I do know, one thing for sure.
With every breath, that I take,
My whole body, really does shake.

I Find It,
"Hard To Breathe"

I find it, hard to breathe,
Just by, looking at you.
I find it, hard to breathe,
When your, eyes meet mine.
I find it, hard to breathe,
Just hearing, your sexy voice.
I find it, hard to breathe,
Cause you are, here by me.
I find it, hard to breathe,
When you are, in my arms.
I find it, hard to breathe,
When your lips, meet mine.
I find it, hard to breathe,
Cause you just, take my breath away.
I find it, hard to breathe,
When I just, think of you.
I find it, hard to breathe,
For all of, the above reasons.
You just make it, hard for me to breathe.

Breathless

I think you are one, of the very best,
Of any and all, of any of the rest.
You have such, a lovable sweetness,
You really have, left me breathless.
Although my heart, was beating fast,
It just stopped, as you sashayed past.
As you walked, with such suredness,
That's what did, leave me breathless.
You made me feel, I ran 100 miles or so,
Girl, I'd follow you, wherever you go.
Standing here my heart, beat with excitedness
That's why it made, me feel so breathless.
If you've had something, like this way,
Then you'd know, what I am trying to say.
All I know is, with all your loveliness,
You have left me, really breathless.

My Stairway To Heaven

TO SOMEONE SPECIAL

I am on, my stairway to heaven,
Cause I'm on my way, to see my angel.
I clmb this, stairway to heaven,
Cause that is, where you are.
You truly are, my special angel,
When I am with you, I am in heaven.
You fill my heart, with heavenly bliss,
Especially when I get, your heavenly kiss.
Your lips are soft, moist, and tender,
And they make, my heart surrender.
Your lips send chills, up and down my spine,
And I feel bubbly, like a sparkling wine.
And when I am, in your warm embrace,
My heart beats, at a faster pace.
That's why I'm on, my stairway to heaven,
Cause I'm on my way, to see my angel.
I climb this, stairway to heaven,
Cause that is, where you are.
I am on, My Stairway To Heaven.

Your Lips, Hair, Smile And You

FOR MY LOVE

Having your soft, moist, lips on mine,
Tastes like a sweet, effervesent wine.
Your lips are so moist, and so sweet,
My lips to yours, they just want to meet.
I run my fingers through, your radiant hair,
Oh my darling, you know, I really care.
You have such, a beautiful, radiant glow,
That really makes me, just love you so.
From the first time, I ever saw you,
I knew that I really, wanted only you.
Your sparkling eyes, and great smile,
Has stayed with me, all this while.
I can think of only, one thing to do,
That's be by your side, and be with you.
You have given me, such a great rise,
My heart has touched, the heavenly skies.
That's why my darling, I want to be with you,
Cause nothing else, will ever, ever do.
For me it's "YOUR LIPS, HAIR, SMILE, AND YOU"

Warmer Weather And I

TO WARMER WEATHER

Warmer Weather is, finally getting here.
It is time to shed, our winter gear.
The days are really, turning fair,
Bright sunshine, and warmer air.
The nights are not, quite as cold,
Night winds not, blowing quite as bold.
Nights getting shorter, we get longer days,
More time for the sunshine's, warmer rays.
Except for Christmas Eve, and Christmas Day,
The cold and snow, can stay away.
Even though kids, love to sled and play,
The aftermath of snow, can really go away.
As for me, I love, the warmer weather,
It makes me feel, as light as a feather.
I love the warm, bright sunshine,
It always makes me, feel just fine.
If you want all, that cold and snow,
Move to Alaska, and become an Eskimo.

Walking Along The Shore

Together as we walk, along the shore,
Arm in arm, loving each other, more and more.

And as we are, walking along,
We're humming, our special song.

We can let our minds, drift into space,
Cause this our, very special place.

We stop, we smile, then a little kiss,
Nothing could ever, be better than this.

As we walk farther, down the shore,
Our hearts are intertwined, even more.

One smile, one kiss, OH, this is heavenly bliss,
From just one, warm and tender kiss.

We are so, very much in love,
Our hearts are floating, in the sky above.

Our hearts keep bonding, even more everyday,
Our love really, and truly, are here to stay.

That's why we walk together, along this shore.

Always Devoted To You!

With your love, I will always abide,
I always want to be, by your side.
I want always, to hold your hand,
I want always, to be your man

I WILL ALWAYS BE, DEVOTED TO YOU!

I will hold you firmly, in my arms,
So you will feel, safe in my arms.
I will give all, my love to you,
Cause I am so, in love with you.

I WILL ALWAYS BE, DEVOTED TO YOU!

You got me hooked, in such a way,
I want to be, with you every day.
I felt it from, the very start,
You have really, captured my heart.

I WILL ALWAYS BE, DEVOTED TO YOU!

My true words, I want you to heed,
No one else, do I, want or need.
My heads spinning, in a whirl,
I need you to be, my only girl.

I WILL ALWAYS BE, DEVOTED TO YOU!

All I Want And Need

MY LOVE

Want to feel your heart, beating next to mine
Beating together, as one, and in perfect time
I want your warm, soft body next to mine
So we can be like this, for all our time.
Won't you please come, and be by my side,
I promise you, I will never, cheat or lie.
When I close my eyes, I see only you,
Day or night, and in my dreams, it is you.
Really don't know, know what to do,
My every thought, is really, about you.
That's why I say, this to you,
This is all I really, want to do.
Want to feel your heart, beating next to mine,
Beating together, as one, and in perfect time
I want your warm, soft body next to mine
So we can be like this, for all our time.
"This Is All, I Want And Need"

As I Sit Here Day Dreaming

TWO LOVES LOST

As I sit here, just daydreaming,
I just feel like, really screaming.
I've had two great loves, in my life,
Now once again, I am without a wife.
Seems like bad luck, always follows me,
I wish I knew why, this has to be.
I gave you a good life, in the beginning,
But then I struck out, in the ninth inning.
We used to joke, laff and play around,
I thought our life, was very sound.
The bad times started, when you went to work,
Now I'm left here alone, like a big ole jerk.
I sit here thinking, about the good times we had,
The wonderful times, before it went bad.
You know it is really, too darn bad,
Cause now I sit here alone, being very sad.
That's why in the midst, of my daydreaming,
I just feel like, really screaming.

As We Look Into Each Others Eyes

There is no, great big surprise.
We are so, in love, with each other,
There really couldn't be, any other.
With a love, that is true and pure,
A warm tender love, that is very sure.
I'm really thrilled, to be with you so much,
I tingle all over, from your soft touch.
It's moments like this, from your warm kiss,
Makes me feel like, I'm in heavenly bliss.
I quiver all over, and my knees are weak,
When we are done, I can hardly speak.
All that comes out, is a little squeek,
I really feel humble, and very meek.
I can't explain, the effect, you have on me,
But no other place, would I, ever want to be.
So, as we look into, each others eyes,
There is no, great surprise.

Be With Me

If ever there was, a certain time,
This is now, for me, that time.
I have wanted you, for oh so long,
I've even sang, it to you, in a song.
Our love just, cannot go wrong,
Cause with me, is where you belong.
I have hoped, and prayed, for this day,
That you'd eventually, come to me this way.
My feelings so far, has carried me thru,
But now it is time, for me to be with you.
The first time I saw, your beautiful face,
My insides shook, my heart started to race.
My feelings inside, I could not hide,
Tho't I went to heaven, tho't I died.
Now that I know, I'm alive, and still here,
Come sweetheart, and be, my loving wife dear.
If ever there was, a certain time,
This is now, for me, that time.

Born To Be With You

TO MY SPECIAL LOVE

Being by, your side,
I'll be, so satisfied.
I'll be so happy, thru and thru,
Cause I was born, to be with you.
These are my feelings, that I can't hide,
Cause I just want, to be by your side.
With a love, that is very true,
Cause I was born, to be with you.
Just to be, here with you,
With a love, that is very true.
To share all, my time with you,
To go thru life, with only you.
Darling this is what, I want to do,
Cause I was born, to be with you.
Wouldn't you love, for me, to be with you?
To share my heart, and my love with you?
I just want to be, by your side,
So we both, can be satisfied.
Cause, ""I was born, to be with you.""

Broken Man

A LOVE LOST!!!!!

As I sit, in my room,
My heart, is full of gloom.
We were together, quite a few years,
Now I sit and shed, a thousand tears.
"Now I am, a Broken Man".
Eveybody thought, that we'd stay together,
Cause we always had, so much fun together.
But now she is gone, forever more,
Cause she has walked, out that door.
"Now I am, a Broken Man".
I knew that she found, someone new,
She said it, wasn't hard to do.
My heart feels, like a sinking ship,
This is a long, sad, and lonely trip.
Can't go forward, can't go back.
I feel I'm on a long, lonely, one way track.
She threw my heart, in a trash can,
"Now I am, a Broken Man".

Deep Feelings

I have a love, burning deep inside,
It's a feeling, I cannot hide.
It yearns so bad, to be set free,
For someone to share, this love with me.
Searching everywhere, for a special love,
I've even looked, towards heaven above.
Searching everywhere, high and low,
Looking and hoping, everywhere I go.
I don't need, a lot of frivolous things,
Just someone to share, the basic things.
Love, Honor, Truth and Honesty,
Are the most, important things to me.
Without these, relationships, are nowhere,
That's why couples, are in such despair.
Can't be true, to your mate, and yourself?
Find a corner, and sit yourself, on a shelf.
I will be loving, and true to thee,
All I ask is that, you be the same to me.

Empty Feeling

As I sit here, looking all around,
Tho't I had my feet, firmly on the ground.
Had my whole world, turned upside down,
That's why I sit here, with a frown.
My last love, I tho't was really the one,
My lonely heart, she surely had won.
We shared, basically everything,
Even exchanged, beautiful wedding rings.
Our love was sent, from up above,
We were OH, so much in love.
So now I sit here, all alone,
In my big lonely, empty home.
When I hear what, was our favorite song,
I try to think of, what went wrong.
As I sit here, with an empty feeling,
My heart really is, still reeling.
She really hurt me, and broke my heart,
When she walked out, and said we had to part.

From Heart To Heart

Holding with love, someone close,
Feel the warmth of, their body close.
Feeling the beating, of each others heart,
In perfect time, with your own heart.
But not having, someone close to you,
Not having their love, to share with you.
I don't think there, could be anything worse
Except maybe your, last ride in a hearse.
My heart has just, been sorely reeling,
And I'm very tired, of this lonely feeling.
I am very tired of all, this loneliness,
I want and need someone, to hold and caress.
Someone sent to me, from up above,
To share with me, my true and open love.
Worldly goods, and things like that,
Is not really, what I'm looking at.
Come let me hold you, and feel our heart,
Beating as one, "From Heart To Heart"

Happy In Love

For me, this is really, no disgrace,
I get all giddy, when I see your lovely face.
You really send, my heart a reelin',
You give me such, a happy feelin'.
I want to hold you, till the end of time,
I want you to know, I'm glad you're mine.
This my darling, I also want you to know,
I'll hold you tight, and never let you go.
The secret of our love, is in your charms,
As I'll forever always, hold you in my arms.
And know this, cause you, now have been told,
I wouldn't trade you, for the worldly gold.
You are, the most important, thing to me,
Without you, where would I be?
With our love, I want to abide,
I always want, to be by your side.
Heaven has given, your love to me,
For, I'm as happy, as can be.

Heavenly Love

The heavenly touch, of your embrace,
Tells me I am, in the right place.
The tender kiss, from your sweet lips,
Brings a smile from, my own hungry lips.
The way you hold me, in your loving arms,
To share with me, your sweet charms.
You have given me, so much love and emotions
I will love you, with all my devotion.
I swear by the moon, and the stars above,
I vow to you, my honest, and true love.
I offer to you my heart, in my hand
I also offer to you, my wedding band.
I want to be with you, always and forever,
I promise that, I'll leave you never.
After we shared, a warm tender kiss,
Then I knew the meaning, of "Heavenly Bliss"
I know it is, as right as it seems,
Cause you are, the girl, of my dreams.

Here I Sit...

Here I sit, all broken hearted,
My love and I, are now departed.
She came home, from work one day,
And told me, I am going away.
I don't know how, things got this way,
For me to know, she did not say.
All I can do, is sit here and pout,
And try to figure, everything out.
She left me here, feelin' kind of dumb,
Not knowing what, I might have done.
To end the beautiful, relationship we had,
Now I'm left here, feeling very sad.
But don't worry, everything will be okay,
I am too strong, to stay this way.
It may take just, a little while,
But one of these days, I'll again smile.
From all of this, I will rise above,
And find myself, another someone to love.
I'll no longer, sit here broken hearted.

I Felt A Tear

FOR ALL WHO REALLY KNOW ME

I stopped and looked, up at the sky,
And I felt something, in my eye.
I tho't it was, a drop of rain,
But it was a tear, from all my pain.
You left me here, to be all alone,
Without anyone, I can call my own.
I have people I talk to, on the phone,
But it don't help, my being here all alone.
You were my loving, dream come true,
Cause I was so very, in love with you.
It was, the thrill, of my life,
When you became, my wife.
But like trash, you threw it away,
When you walked out, and left me that day.
You found someone else, to take my place,
And now you are living, in another place.
But don't worry, I'll survive some way,
And find another love, for me some day.

I Give My Heart To You

I'm in a bit, of a quandry,
Cause I am, in love with thee.
I am in a bit, of confusion it seems,
Cause you have been, the girl of my dreams.
Together is what, I want us to be,
No one else, in this world, just you and me.
I wasn't up for, any kind of tricks,
But this hit me, like a ton of bricks.
My heart left me, and went straight to you,
And said to me, it was in love with you.
Now I don't know, just what to do,
Cause I am so, in love with you.
We started out together, just a talking,
Then my heart to you, just went walking.
Now my heart is, no longer mine,
It wants to be, with you, for all time.
I can't really argue, with my heart,
So I give you, my soul, and my heart.
""I GIVE MY HEART TO YOU""

I Got You In My Mind

It's only us, that really knows,
Why I give you, this heart and rose.
You're very special, in my heart,
You've been there, from the very start.
You're friendship, I really care,
You're friendship, I want to share.
You're so sweet, and so very kind,
That's why, I got you, in my mind.
It's kind of funny, that's for sure,
I fell in love, with your picture.
It's too bad we can't, meet some place,
So we could really, meet face to face.
I have no way right now, to come see you,
So I guess this way, will just have to do.
To tell you what, I want to tell you.
That I'd very much, like to be with you.
Cause, "I got you in my mind."

I Need Your Love

Kicking back, and sitting, and wondering,
My insides are, just a floundering.
Something to me, really does haunt,
There is one girl, that I really want.
Can't make her see, she means the world to me
She honestly does, mean the world to me.
There's nothing that, I wouldn't, do for her,
Everything within me, would be just for her.
I'm afraid it's not me, she feels she needs.
But I would beg, down on a bended knee.
If you would please, come and be with me,
A better life I promise, I would give thee.
Here is something, I want you to believe,
I need your love, as well as I breathe.
As well as any substance, I need to live,
All my love and attention, to you I'll give.
No other girl, has made me, feel this way,
I love you is all, that I need you to say,
I NEED YOUR LOVE.

I Never Knew

I never knew how much, I love you,
Until I spent some, time with you.
We joked, and laffed, and played around,
Then one day my heart, started to pound.
I thought it was, from playing around,
But this time it had, a different sound.
It never felt, or sounded, like this before,
It just made me drop, down to the floor.
As I sat there and, was looking about,
I LOVE YOU, I LOVE YOU, I wanted to shout.
But I didn't know, if you felt the same,
And that would've been, a real shame.
But now I'm happy, what you said to me,
You said you would, be happy to be with me.
For me it was like, a real rebirth,
Cause I am, the happiest man, here on earth.
Now I have a love, of my very own,
Because of the way, our love has grown.
I never knew before, how much, I loved you.

I Promise

I promise to love you, with all my might,
Everyday, every morning, noon, and night.
I promise to hold you, lovingly in my arms,
And reveal to you, all my loving charms.
I promise to hold you, if you sit and sigh,
And hold you lovingly, if you need to cry.
I promise to be there, for your every need,
I'll be there with my, every tho't and deed.
I promise to always, wipe away your tears,
From now and for, the rest of your years.
I promise my dear, to never lie to you,
And I never, ever, will cheat on you.
I promise I will, love only you,
Cause my love, is only for you.
I promise always, to try, to be by your side,
Even through lifes, sometimes bumpy ride.
So I promise to give, my life, just for you,
Cause I am so deeply, madly, in love with you
These things to you, "I PROMISE"

I Want You

The smell of your fragrance, as I walk by,
Makes my heart pound, as I walk by.
The smile on your, lovely face,
Makes me do, an about face.
I just have to, come back to you,
And sincerely have, a talk with you.
I have had, a very long, and lonely life,
But now I know how, to cheer up my life.
There is no mysterious, or fancy rhyme,
I just want to, make you all mine.
Just give me, some kind, of a sign girl,
Cause you have, set my heart, in a whirl.
There is one thing, that there is no doubt,
You make my heart, soar above the clouds.
If you say that, you will be be mine,
I'll love and cherish, you for all time.

If Ever There Would Be

If ever there would be, someone just for me,
You are the one, who I would want it to be.
With your sweet, and lovely charms,
I'll hold you forever, in my arms.
The soft tender touch, of your warm embrace,
I wouldn't want to be, in any other place.
And this dear girl, I want you to believe,
I cherish the air, that you breathe.
Every breath, that you take every day,
Keeps you here for me, another day.
I didn't care, what happened to me,
You have given, a renewed life to me.
So you see, my dear loved one,
There couldn't be, no other one.
If ever there would be, someone just for me,
You would be the only one, I'd want it to be.

I'M So Sad

It is really, so very sad,
The misfortunes, that I've had.
Can't seem to find, someone just for me,
Someone who will, love just me.
I have tried, oh, so many times,
Thru my lines, and their loving rhymes.
And as many times, I have entered my plea,
No one has come forth, to be with me.
I really don't know, what else to do,
I am breathless, from asking for you.
Where oh where, are you my love?
Or do you just need, a little shove?
Maybe the love Angel, can send you my way,
And really make this, my happy day.
Oh how I hunger, for such heavenly bliss,
Of someones warm, and tender kiss.
I want to feel, warm and alive,
In the New Year, of 2005.

In Our Loving Arms

TO SOMEONE SPECIAL

As I sit here, on the floor,
With my back, against the door.
I like to ponder, without a doubt,
How to keep, everyone else out.
But I get this feeling, from deep within,
And I don't want to let, anyone else in.
As you hold my heart, in your hand,
You make me feel, oh so grand.
This special feeling, makes us glow,
As we make love, oh so slow.
You give my body, such a feeling,
It gets my heart, rocking and reeling.
I get this feeling, from deep inside,
Makes me want, to curl up, with you and hide.
This is where, I want to be,
Cause in your arms, I feel free.
Cause with you, I want to be,
In this world, just you and me.

THIS WAS CO-WRITTEN BY MY GIRLFRIEND AND I BEFORE
WE WERE MARRIED, NOW MY EX.

It Is Again
The Time Of Year

WINTER AND KIDS!!!!!

Time to shed all, our summer gear.
The time, of the changing weather,
Time to wear, our coats and sweaters.
Time to start having, shorter days,
Having longer nights, from day to day.
Blustery winds, and dark grey skies,
And the cold, as the snow flies.
Time to have, snow covered places,
As the snow, and the wind hit our faces.
Kids will face all of this, big and bold,
They are not afraid, of the cold.
They will frolic, and play in the snow,
You will see this, everywhere you go.
Sliding and, riding, their sleds,
No other tho'ts, are in their heads.
Do you remember, as a kid, this kind of day?
When you had fun, in this kind of way?
It's again, the time of year

My Love For You

My love for you, is as big as the sky,
And do you, want to know why?
You are so warm, soft, and lovely,
No other place, would I want to be.
Just the touch of, your warm embrace,
Sends me deep, into outer space.
I glide around the stars, and the moon,
You have made, my poor heart swoon.
Your eyes sparkle, like the stars above,
That is why, I am, so much in love.
Your hair has such, a radiant shine,
It makes me so glad, that you are mine.
Your lips are red, moist, and soft too,
They make me tremble, when I kiss you.
You have made my heart, melt inside,
It's such a love, that I cannot hide.
Heaven has given, this love, to me and you,
We will continue, this love, in heaven too.
This Is, My Love For You.

My Fate

I guess it's, just my fate,
To live here alone, without a mate.
Several times, I have tried,
And several times, I have sat and cried.
Just when I think, I have found someone,
They end up being, someone else's someone.
Life used to be, really great,
I used to have, a beautiful mate.
We shared love, and had fun for awhile,
Then they just leave, with a little smile.
I sit back wondering, what went wrong,
Especially when I hear, our favorite song.
This is one of life's, Dastardly Deeds,
Seems like someone else, always intercedes.
I try to give them, my whole heart,
They stay for awhile, then they depart.
So I guess it's, just my fate,
To live here alone, without a mate.

My Head

My heads going, up and down,
And spinnin', round and round.
Since the first time, that I looked at you,
I don't know what, I'm a gonna do.
Bouncin' up and down, like a rubber ball,
Never felt like this, that I can recall.
Spinning round and round, like a giant top,
I think the damn thing, is gonna pop.
As you walked by, into the setting sun,
I knew that you, had to be, my special one.
You were looking, so good and fine,
Like a regal, bubbly, sparkling wine.
You set my heart, and my head, in a whirl,
I knew, I had to, make you my girl.
Heads going up and down, like a rubber ball,
Up and down so hard, I just might fall.
Round and round so fast, like a giant top,
I think that it, just might pop.

Love For You

You are the apple, of my eye,
My love for you, is as big, as the sky.
I never wanted, anyone but you,
No one else, would ever do.
You are my one, and only, true love,
You were sent to me, from up above.
No man has ever, had a greater love,
My love for you, is a very special love.
I can't eat, work, or even sleep,
Cause somehow in my mind, you always creep.
My every thought is, really about you,
It makes me happy, I'm in love with you.
There is something that, I need from you,
I really have to know, if you love me too.
Then I'd know, you were sent, from the sky,
And then I'd be, the worlds, happiest guy.
Cause you are, the apple, of my eye,
My love for you, is as big, as the sky.

My Soul and My Heart

I give you my soul, and my heart,
And a Love, that will never part.
I've known it, from the very start,
You have won, my lonely heart.
From the first time, that I saw you,
I knew I wanted, to be with you.
I can't think of, anyone but you,
No one else, would ever do.
I give my heart to you, in my hand,
Our Love will be, OH so grand.
So, my soul and my heart, I offer you,
Let me share, my Love with you.
I will Love, and cherish you,
With my whole being, thru and thru.

Oh Wow! Just Look At That Beautiful Sky!

Oh wow! Just look at that beautiful sky,
Isn't that, a beautiful sight.
Such a colorful display, for one's eyes,
Day is fading, into twilight,
It's the close, of another day,
The red, pink, blue, and the purple too.
The colorful hue, from the setting sun's rays,
Such an exquisite display, for me and you.
Day is turning, into the night,
The sky now giving us, a different view.
It will be dark, very soon,
As the sun disappears, from our view.
We will then see, the stars and the moon,
That is why I say,
Oh wow! Just look at, that beautiful sky!

Our Love Was Planned

Together, I planned, we will always will be,
Cause I love you, and you love me.
I loved you from, the very start,
You are the one girl, who stole my heart.
I vowed, my love for you, would always be,
From the beginning, and thru all eternity.
You really make, my heart beam,
You are the one girl, of my dreams.
I have planned, and I have schemed,
For you, to come to me, out of my dreams.
One look at, your beautiful face,
Had me floating, up in outer space.
With the eagles, you had me soaring,
With you, life has been, anything but boring.
I never walk around, with a frown,
You have me acting, like a funny clown.
It's a new, and wonderful, feeling for me,
This is how, it was planned, for you and me.

Please Be Mine

Twiddle dee dee, twiddle dee dum,
Look out woman, here I come.
I have my heart, here in my hand,
Do not take it, with a grain of sand.
I will be honest, and true to you,
In everything, that I say and do.
All I want to do, is be with you,
The rest of my life, just be with you.
You have made my, whole body tingle,
I am so very tired, of being single.
The blood in my body, is just a-pumpin',
My poor heart is really, jumpin' and thumpin'.
Please tell me, that you'll be mine,
Or I will sit here, and just whine.
If you don't tell me, that you'll be mine,
I'll sit and whine, till the end of time.

Walking, Coming Towards Me

As I watch you walk, coming my way,
You're fluid steps, and hips that sway,
And a great big smile, upon your face,
Tells me I am here, in the right place.
I like to watch you, wiggle and shake,
And that tells me, you are not a fake.
You are my living, and breathing fantasy,
I love to watch you, come towards me.
You are so sweet, and so very lovely,
I want you to be mine, please come with me.
Nothin' would be better, that I would love,
Than you being my sweet, true turtle dove.
Girl you are always, in my every thoughts,
Baby for you, I really have got the hots.
You really make, my insides, turn inside out,
And sweetheart, believe this, without doubt.
I really want, you to be, my very own,
Come with me and share, my lonely home.
I love to watch you, "walking, coming my way."

What You Have Done For Me

What you have, done for me,
Is really pure, sweet poetry.
You have really, shown to me,
How sweet and good, love can be.
You have lifted, my heart high above,
With your warm, and tender love.
You have also, shown me, how to care,
And with my love, how to share.
I was just, a very lonesome heart,
You captured my heart, from the start.
From the first time, that I saw you,
I knew that I was, in love with you.
Wow, now you know, that I feel good,
And being with you, I knew that I would.
Now with you, I really, feel so secure
You've given, my lonely heart a cure.
It's really like, pure poetry,
What you have, done for me.

When I Look Into Your Eyes

When I look, into your eyes
I see the same blue, that's in the sky.
The sparkling in your eyes, are so sharp,
I hear the Angels, playing their harps.
Your eyes are so clear, and so bright,
They even sparkle, in the dead of night.
Your eyes are so beautiful, and very blue,
They are like pool water, they're icy blue.
I could dive in there, and get lost in you,
And stay in there forever, cause I love you.
You're awesome feature, is your eyes shine,
And for that, I am happy, that you are mine.
When I look into, your big blue eyes,
I feel like I'm soaring, through the sky.
Gliding through the heavens, high above,
Like on the wings, of a pure white dove.
For me this is, a delightful surprise,
When I look, into your deep blue eyes.

When We Met

TO SOMEONE SPECIAL

We talked awhile, on line,
And everything has, been just fine.
We got along good, with each other,
Then we decided, to meet each other.
A lovely surprise, it turned out to be,
And it was better, than I tho't it'd be.
My dear sweet, darling girl,
You kind of set, my heart in a whirl.
And when we met, face to face,
It turned out, to be, a magical place.
You were a bit, of a surprise to me,
I didn't know, how much fun, you could be.
We didn't have time, to go out anywhere,
But we had fun, just right there.
You showed me a side, that I didn't know,
And I am sure, that it did show.
But at nite, morning, or at noon,
I'd like, to do this, again soon.
JUST TO SEE YOU

Why Does Life Have To Be So Cruel?

FOR A LOVE I THO'T WAS MINE ALONE!!

"Why does life, have to be so cruel?"
I have always tried, not to be a fool.
I met a girl who, set, my heart awhirl,
I knew I really, had, to have that girl.
I felt that life, was really sublime,
We were in love, for a long, long time.
Both of our hearts, were beating as one,
We always had, so much fun.
"Why does life, have to be so cruel?"
It really made me, feel, like a fool.
She met someone else, to take my place,
She couldn't even tell, me, to my face.
"Why does life, have to be so cruel?"
I tho't our love, was doing just fine,
Tho't we'd stay, together, all the time.
But in the end, she found a new boyfriend,
That was the, beginning, of the end.
"Why does life, have to be so cruel?"

With Love In Our Hearts

My coming home, late from work,
I crawl in bed, beside you very carefully.
So as not to, wake you up, from your sleep,
I prop myself up, on my elbow, watching you.
You are so beautiful, sleeping very restfully,
I stroke your cheek, softly with my fingers.
And so very lightly, over your face,
Somehow I know, you know, in your sleep.
Cause you give, a little hmm, and a smile,
And that makes me, feel good, and very happy.
So I snuggle up, and put my arm around you,
And you put my hand, against your heart.
I feel the the soft, rhythmic, slow beating,
Being with you, like this, makes me happy.
That's why, I am so much, in love with you,
I nestle my head, into your neck softly.
And I whisper ever so softly, I love you,
And you answer back, I love you too.
We both go to sleep, With Love In Our Hearts.

Words From My Heart

With each poem, that I start,
They always come, from my heart.
Some are from, loves gone bad,
And that makes me, so doggone sad.
A few are about ones, that were good for me,
I try, to express them this way, you see?
Others are about, ones, I wish I had,
This also makes me, kind of sad.
Some are said, in kind of, a funny way,
Laffing words are, what I try to say.
But all of them have, a certain meaning,
Some may have your eyes, mistily gleaming.
But my personal want, and hopeful need,
Is to have you enjoy them, as you read.
So, as you read them, from the start,
Remember, that they come, from my heart.

You Are Always On My Mind

You are so very, sweet and kind,
You are always, on my mind.
I can't think of, anything but you,
You're on my mind, thru and thru.
Even when I go, to sleep at night,
A picture of you, comes into sight.
Can't wait to see, your smiling face today,
When I wake up, to face a brand new day.
When I'm at work, I always get behind,
Cause you are, always on my mind.
I can't relax, eat, work, or sleep,
Cause into my mind, you always creep.
Even if I go, to some kind, of sports game,
Somehow I always seem, to hear your name.
If I go out for some fun, at some bar,
Still in my mind, there you are.
No matter what, I try to say or do,
Someone always, has to mention you,
That's why you are, always on my mind.

I Never Tho'T

I never tho't, I'd get caught again,
Not ever again, in a hundred years.
But you touched my heart, in such a way,
That gave it a spark, and came alive again.
And it knows that it is, in love once more,
And as a matter of fact, so do I.
You have affected me, in a strange way,
That I really, and truly, cannot explain.
I only know, one thing for sure,
You have turned, my heart, upside down.
Now I no longer walk, around with a frown,
Now I have nothing, but happy smiles.
A complete turnaround, you have made me do,
Cause a new love, in you, I have found.
I was really ready, to give it all up,
Then all of a sudden, there you are.
So now I can, love only you,
From here, to where, you are.
""I Never Tho't, I'd Get Caught again""

I Offer You

I offer to you, my hand,
So we can walk, hand in hand.
I also offer, to you, my heart,
I fell in love, from the start.
Cause of me, you took control,
And I offer you, my very soul.
Next to mine, I want your heart,
To beat as one, with my heart.
I offer also, my life to you,
I just want, to be with you.
I offer all these, things to you
Cause I am so, in love with you.
I offer to you, my hand,
So we can walk, hand in hand.
I offer to you, my very soul,
Cause of me, you took control.
I also offer, to you, my heart,
I fell in love, from the start.
These things, "I OFFER YOU".

I Really Am In Love With You

I want you, I want you, I want you to know,
That I really am, so much, in love with you.
Nothing else matters, to me anynore,
Except that I, will love you forevermore.
Please say that you, will be only mine,
So I can love only you, for all time.
My eyes opened wide, just looking at you,
That's when I knew, I was in love with you.
You really have set, my heart on fire,
It was like grabbing, a real live wire.
Watching you walk, with that swish and sway
Also made me fall, in love with you that day
My heart really fell, down at your feet,
You're the only girl, that I wanted to meet
And this is true, without a doubt,
My insides were, turned inside out.
This is why I say, this just to you,
I want you, I want you, I want you to know,
I really am so much, "IN LOVE WITH YOU".

I Want To Hold You, In My Arms

I want to hold you, in my arms,
I want to hold you, so warm and tender.
Your ear I want to, whisper sweet nothins',
Sweet words that, you love to hear.
I also want to, nibble on your ear,
But don't worry, cause I don't bite.
I want to kiss, your neck, so fair,
And give you, a tender kiss, on your lips.
I want to stroke, your hair, soft and silky,
And get a whiff, of your awesome fragrance.
Which give me thrills, of withering heights
And the pressure of, your body next to mine
Make me lose, all conception of time,
I feel like, I am floating, among the stars
Honey, when your body, is next to mine,
I am filled with, such sweet exstacy.
I want to hold you, in my arms,
So all our charms, we can savor.
"I want to hold you, in my arms."

I Would Walk

I would walk, these distant miles,
Just to see, your lovely smiles.
And to be able, to kiss your sweet lips,
Caress you tenderly, with my fingertips.
To hold you lovingly, in my arms,
To be able to share, our loving charms.
I'll run my fingers, lightly thru your hair,
Just to show you, that I truly care.
I would surely walk, these distant miles,
To show you that, my love, is worthwhile.
I would do, all these things, just for you,
To show you that, my love, for you is true.
Thru my tribulations, and all my trials,
These would be, my happiest, walking miles.
I'd walk to the end, of the earth, for you,
Just to prove, my love, is only for you.
I would walk, these distant miles,
So we could share, our loving smiles.

I'd Find You !!

Even though you live, pretty far away,
There is something, that I must say.
No matter timewise, and how far,
I'll follow that one, little twinkling star.
It wouldn't seem to be, all that far,
Cause it'll lead me, to where you are.
Then we'd be able, to meet face to face,
Then maybe a little hug, and a warm embrace.
My nerves would be, somewhere in outerspace,
My heart would feel like, it's been in a race
Nothing can compare, with the feeling inside,
I would greet you with, my arms open wide.
So you see, you are not, all that far away,
For me to come see you, one fine day.
No matter what, may come our way,
We have met, we can always say.
Nothing would give me, greater pleasure,
Cause I just might find, my greatest treasure
I'D FIND YOU !!

If I Was Laying Next To You

If I was laying, next to you,
Do you know, what I would do?
I would hold you tenderly, in my arms,
I would caress you, from head to toes.
I would run my fingers, thru your hair,
So soft and shiny, and very radiant.
I'd caress your face, so soft and creamy,
And blow in your ear, so very softly.
I'd run my fingers, softly all over you,
Till you wouldn't, know what to do.
I would make you, moan and groan,
With anticipation, and excitement,
Cause I am so much, in love with you.
I want to give you, so much pleasure,
With every inch, of you, that I touch.
I would have you wanting, all my love,
This is everything, that I would do.
If I was, laying next to you.

If It Wasn't For You

If it wasn't for, someone like you,
I don't know what, I would do.
I've just about given up, on any love,
But you changed, my mind about love.
I've been bumming, around feeling sad,
But you showed me, all is not bad.
I've gotten away, from all this strife,
And I'm starting, to see a better life.
Now and then, we all need, a little shove,
To help find, someone else to love.
Because you are so sweet, and very kind,
For awhile I've had you, on my mind.
I would do anything, in the world for you,
All you'd really have to do, is ask me to.
Make my life complete, come stay with me,
I'll show you how, my love really could be.
No promises I'll make you, except for one,
I'll love you till, our lives will be done.

If You Would, Come With Me

If you would, come with me,
I would, love you faithfully.
You are, my hearts desire,
Like touching, a live wire.
I feel the sparks, from your heart,
Hitting me right, in my own heart.
I just want, to really say,
You bring joy, and sunshine my way.
You really just, light up my day,
And you do it, to me every day.
With the loving words, that you say,
And send to me, lovingly, every day.
I want to make you, my very own,
And make this, a very happy home.
I really felt it, from the very start,
You have captured, my lonely heart.
If you would, come with me,
I will love you, faithfully.
If you would, "COME WITH ME"

Just Thinking Of You

When I sit, and think of you,
My feelings just really, go loop de loo.
And my thoughts give, me a heck of a rush,
And my insides really, just turn to mush.
No other girl, has taken me this far,
The top of my list, is where you are.
You are way up there, up above,
Don't want anyone else, to share my love.
My heart belongs, to no one but you,
My love is unconditional, thru and thru.
Some other girls, I may see,
But it's you, I want for me.
With your charm, and lovely personality,
Is the only place, that I want to be.
You opened my eyes, and my heart,
It was only you, from the start.
I know now, no others, will ever do,
Cause I am hopelessly, in love with you.

Looking For A New Love

Laying in bed last nite, looking at the sky,
There was one star, bright way up high.
It was just there, at me clearly winking,
Got me to start, wondering and thinking.
About the things I have, and don't have,
But the one thing, that I really don't have.
Is someone to have, hold, and to love,
Someone to share with me, all my love.
To be loved I'd give, my worldly things,
To again have happiness, true love brings.
I almost had the girl, that I really loved,
She would have been, my true beloved.
But something went wrong, and she went away,
And since then, I've been blue, every day.
No matter what, may come my way,
I'll keep searching, every day.
Why can't someone be, sent from up above,
Someone special whom wants, to share a love.

My Chance Meeting

Wow, yesterday was, certainly quite a day,
I must really, just have to say.
As I was walking, down the street,
A cute little girl, did I meet.
She smiled at me, and said hi,
I smiled back, and returned her hi.
We slowed down, and watched each other,
More or less just, sizing up each other.
The sun and wind, was giving us fits,
But we talked, about fifteen minutes.
She asked me and, I gave her my number,
To call me but I doubt, she'd even remember.
Talk about a nice, charming meeting,
But thanks to her, and our, morning meeting.
All I can tell you, I'm as happy as can be,
Maybe I really, found a girl, just for me.
All I can think of, is her smiling face,
And her nice warm, and tender embrace.
Then the stupid, alarm clock, woke me up.

My Heart Knew It Was You

This is a fact, and it is no baloney,
I am tired of, being lonely.
I just need someone, to hold and love,
Won't you come to me, and share my love?
When you walked, coming towards me,
You looked like a, beautiful goddess to me.
The way you smiled, as you walked along,
Humming and singing, some kind of song.
I knew there was, definitely something wrong.
Cause my heart hit bottom, like a giant gong.
Seeing your hair, eyes, your sensous lips,
Made me want to do, some backward flips.
You made my heart just stop, and skip a beat,
I darn near fainted, there in the street.
You gave me a feeling, I can't describe,
When my heart stopped, I tho't it just died.
That's when I knew, I was in love with you,
Cause my heart also told me, it was you.

My Hopeful One

I've been talking to a girl, for awhile now,
And I am interested, about her and how.
She seems very kind, and very sweet,
A very nice girl, who I did meet.
I have met her, here on line,
She seems to be, just so fine.
I'd like her to come, and stay with me,
And show her how, a good life could be.
In a sentence she said, she was intrigued,
But I am also really, very much intrigued.
She is the one who, has come so close,
And I am leaning towards, her the most.
My heart has really, just gone oooweee,
She has kindled, a little fire in me.
If it would work out, and she'd be my girl,
I'd be the happiest guy, in this world.
Please say you will, come and stay with me,
I'll share every ounce, of love, within me.

My Life And Love, I Offer To You

I made up my mind, To really strive,
To not give in, and to stay alive.
Cause I still have, a life to live,
And have a lot, of love, still to give.
This is written, to you, in my song,
My hearts been lonely, for too long.
Some of my loves, have gone wrong,
But my heart still has, love so strong.
I want to give, and share, my love with you,
And I will be loyal, and true, to only you.
I want someone to share, my love with me,
And you are the one, that I want it to be.
You have instilled, a new life in me,
I no longer, want to be, sad and lonely.
So now, that you know, what I mean,
Come be with me, and be my Queen.
Cause I still, have a lot, of life to live,
And still have, a lot of love to give.
"MY LIFE AND LOVE, I OFFER TO YOU."

My Love Is Only For You

You are the girl, I have been waiting for,
You are the one, that I love and adore.
It was like seeing you, on a picture screen,
I have seen you, in all of my dreams.
You made my heart stop, and skip a beat,
When I saw you walking, down the street.
You are so very lovely, and so very sweet,
My heart just fell, right down, at your feet.
Then with our first, warm and tender embrace,
My heart felt like it was, in a long race.
But even though it kept, beating this fast,
I wanted this feeling, to always last.
Must have been witchcraft, what you did to me
Cause you put a wicked, love spell on me.
Now, heaven is here, down on earth for me.
Because you are now, here beside me.
All my love, I do pledge, only for you,
Forever and ever, my love, is only for you.
"THIS IS, MY LOVE FOR YOU".

My Online Mate

There is a girl, I've been talking to,
And she seems to be, very sweet too.
We just started talking, here on line,
And everything seems, to be just fine.
So she has become, my online mate,
And we are having, an online date.
A lot in common, do we have too,
Amazing and nice, this is too.
We've talked, and teased, and also joked,
Had me laffing so hard, I almost choked.
She's looking for, the same thing as me,
Maybe this could be, the girl just for me.
We both just have, been wandering around,
Maybe we can put, our feet back on the ground
I hope we can continue, to have our fun,
And come together, and be as one.
We have gotten off, to a great start,
To have and hold, I offer you my heart.

My Thoughts Of You

If ever there would be, a girl for me,
You are the one, that it would be.
From all the other girls, that I have seen,
I want you really, to be my queen.
We fit together, like the hand and glove,
I know it is you, that I truly love.
Your eyes sparkle, like an effervesent wine,
I want you to be with me, for all our time.
Your lips look so, moist and sweet,
My lips to yours, just want to meet.
Your hair has such, a beautiful radiant glow,
They are a few things, that make me love you so.
All I can do right now, is imagine your face,
And think about a nice, warm loving embrace.
Do you think, the same things about me?
And how our lives, could really be?
Time will really tell, how it will be.
All I know is that, I really love thee.

Needed: Someone To Love

Where is that someone, somewhere just for me?
That someone to share my love, just with me.
How I long to find, that special love,
The one to be my own, special turtle dove.
I have been searching, high and low,
Stopping and searching, everywhere I go.
I have had a few, who have come to me,
But they have decided, they want to be free.
Why can't I find, that one true love?
One who wants, a one woman mans love.
I need someone, to be, here with me,
I'm so lonely here, by myself, don't you see?
I just want to be happy, the rest of my life,
You don't even, have to be, my loving wife.
It would be really, oh so great,
If you'd just be, my loving mate.
I am not that very hard, to really please,
Just someone to love, and hug and squeeze.
NEEDED: SOMEONE, TO LOVE.

No One Has To Live Sad And All Alone

Here I sit alone, drinkin' beer,
Sad over the one, that I loved so dear.
Everytime I go, to visit her grave,
I think about the love, for me she gave.
We've both been thru, good times and bad,
That's why losing her, makes me so sad.
I can't keep going, on this way,
But I know, God has plans, for me today.
I've felt in mine, his loving hand,
I follow his footprints, in the sand.
On this path I have, followed him to see,
To where it is, that he wants, me to see.
On the shore was a girl, looking over the sea
All of a sudden, she stopped, and looked at me
Her smile, and her eyes, made my heart pound,
I heard beautiful, heavenly music, all around.
Then I knew, what was, meant for me,
God, and my love, wanted to see, me be happy.

*THIS WAS CO-WRITTEN BY ME AND MY EX-FRIEND JON
WHEN WE WERE STILL FRIENDS.*

Offering You My Heart

All I can offer you, is my heart,
Cause you have, stolen my heart.
From the first day, that I saw you,
I knew I was, in love with you.
And now the heavenly touch, of your embrace,
I know no one could ever, take your place.
And the beauty of, your angelic face
I don't want to be, in any other place.
And your soft, light golden hair,
Just leaves me gasping, for more air.
Your eyes that sparkle, in the sunlight,
Makes the sun shine, with a brighter light.
And the way you walk, with such style,
All I can do, is watch with a smile.
You really have given me, a brighter life,
Instead of being here, in this life of strife.
I'm so glad that, I have made you mine,
So we can be happy, and in love, for all time.

Oh, How I Yearn

I'm cruisin' along, with no place to go,
I see all, the pretty girls, walking by.
I get a very, empty feeling inside,
How I wish, I could have one, to be mine.
They all look, at me, and smile,
Some of them, even look and wave.
And that, even makes, me feel worse,
Cause they will go, home to someone else.
And I know when, my ride is done,
I will go home, to an empty house.
You see, I have no one, waiting for me,
It's just, my two cats, and me.
My computer and tv, keeps me company,
But that's better than, staring, at my walls.
Oh, how I yearn, to share my love,
And yearn to be, loved in return.
In this whole, great big world,
I have only one, great big wish.
I yearn for someone, to love me.

Only The Two Of Us

If in this world, there would be,
Just the two of us, only you and me.
Do you think we, would get along?
Walking together, humming a song?
Just you and me, cruising this land,
Or just strolling along, hand and hand.
I couldn't think of, another place to be,
Where it wouldn't be, just you and me.
When I look in your eyes, it's heaven I see,
Cause you are, a blessing to me.
Our two hearts, beating as one,
Since our love, has truly begun.
You for me, and me for you,
Is all I've ever, wanted from you.
Now that we, have become one,
We'll share our lives, under the moon and sun.
"ONLY THE TWO OF US"

Satisfied

When I'm walking with you, by your side,
I'm so very happy, and very satisfied.
Cause you are my, one and only true love,
Of any other girls, you are the one above.
I fell for you, like a ton of falling bricks
And I fell without, any kind of tricks.
You really make my heart, just go crazy,
My mind and my tho'ts, are just so hazy.
With any other girl, I don't want to be,
Cause I'm satisfied, having you with me.
I have waited for you, for a long time,
And I am satisfied, that you are mine.
"Roses are red, and violets are blue,
I am happy to be, in love with you,
Sugar is sweet, and so are you.
That is why I am, so in love with you."
Can't you see and, really tell,
You have me completely, under your spell.

Searching

M,TU,W,TH,F,S,SU, everyday of the week,
Searching for a love, is what I seek.
Someone to hold, and hug, and to love,
Someone to share with me, all my love.
I don't ask for a lot, of worldly things
Just someone to wear, my wedding ring.
From all the rest, I'd put you above,
If with me you would, accept my love.
This would be, my biggest pleasure,
Cause you'd be, my greatest treasure.
Nothing else would be, important to me,
Every ounce of my love, I'd give to thee
I've searched hi and lo, and in between
But so far, you have not, been seen.
Why are you, hiding away from me?
I need your love, OH, don't you see?
Won't you please come, and take my hand
I don't want to die, being a lonely man.

She Drives Me Crazy

There is a girl, and her name isn't Daisy,
But this girl really, drives me crazy.
Every time I look at her, I fall apart,
I can't seem to calm down, my pounding heart
I become such a shaking, nervous wreck,
My head feels like a volcano, above my neck.
My heart still beats, but it feels like mush
She really gives me, a tremendous rush.
Palms sweaty, I'm all jittery, knees very weak
As I try to speak, I just get, a little squeek
Her eyes are big, and clear and bright,
They shine in, any kind of light.
Her eyes are, a genuine prize,
She has beautiful, and sparkling eyes.
Her hair is radiant, and glistens in the sun,
You really know, she is a special one.
I really don't have, any kind of clue,
Why she makes me, feel the way I do.
All I know is, she really drives me crazy.

Sleepless Nights

The wee hours of, the morning are bad for me.
I have trouble sleeping, sometimes don't you see
As I lay there trying, to fall back to sleep,
I see your face, instead of falling to sleep.
It is a very happy, and pleasant sight
But it keeps me up, most of the night.
Some people say, I am some kind of a jerk,
Cause I am so tired, when I go to work.
When I do sleep, my dreams are about you,
I just can't seem, to let go of you.
I really don't know how, to deal with this,
Especially after getting, a tender kiss.
My love for you just, keeps on brewing,
It's got me so, I don't know, what I'm doing.
So now it's time, to wake up, and try to find
A way to keep you, out of my mind.
But my tho'ts will be, here again tonight
And they will be again, an awesome sight.

So Happy To See You

When you're near, my heart wants to fly.
All the way up, into the clear blue sky.
It beats so hard, and very rapidly,
It just wants to go, to you from me.
I will tell you, you got to, my poor heart,
Cause I really fell for you, from the start.
My heart went to you, and went wild,
Like a poor little, hungry child.
Every time, that I see you,
I just can't hide, my feelings for you.
You have me acting, like a goofy clown,
When you're not around, all I do is frown.
But when I see you, my face lights up,
And I act like a little, tail wagging pup.
I am so happy, to see you
I'd do any kind, of tricks for you.
But now that I have, made you mine,
I'll the happiest man, till the end of time.
Cause I am, "SO HAPPY TO SEE YOU."

Sometimes

Sometimes I get, to clowning around,
Sometimes I want, to crawl in the ground.
Sometimes I get happy, then I get sad,
Somethimes I am congenial, then I get mad.
Sometimes my feelings, are hard to explain,
Sometimes I am, in a lot of pain.
Sometimes I am full, of a lot fun,
Sometimes I feel like saying, I am done.
Sometimes I feel, the world is against me,
Cause I don't have, a love here beside me.
Sometimes I really feel, just like dying,
Cause I am just, so tired of crying.
I have cried, a couple thousand tears,
Over the past few, and sad lonely years.
Sometimes I get, to feeling very lucky,
Then it turns around, and I get unlucky.
Sometimes this world, just isn't fair,
Cause I can't find, someone to really care.
SOMETIMES.

Star Light, Star Bright

FOR MY FAMILY AND FRIENDS

Starlight, star bright, first star I see tonite,
Wish I may, wish I might, have this wish tonite
I wish I had, someone to hold, and to love,
Someone sent, just for me, from up above.
I will hold her, and love her, very dearly,
Cause I'm tired, of being alone and weary.
I just want to make, this a happy home,
Cause I'm tired, of being sad and alone.
Won't you grant me, this wish that I ask?
I know for you, it is, no great big task.
I promise to her, to be honest and true,
In everything that, I say and do.
I will love her, with all my heart,
And vow to her, I will never depart.
She will be the center, of my whole being,
All my love to her, I will bring.
Starlight, star bright, first star I see tonite
Wish I may, wish I might, have this wish tonite

The Feel Of Your Body

I am happy, with you right now,
But I'd be, a lot happier.
To feel the warmth, of your body,
To smell the fragrance, of your body.
To feel the softness, of your hair,
And to feel the beating, of your heart.
Beating softly, against mine,
Just holding you, tenderly in my arms.
Sharing our love, and our charms,
The chill of night, holding tighter.
The close warmth, of our bodies,
Standing together, being face to face.
As I run my fingers, across your face,
Inhaling the smell, of your body wash.
Making my whole body, fill with desire,
I just want to hold you, the nite thru.
I just love you, the way you are,
You truly are, my heavenly girl.
I wouldn't trade you, for the world.

The Fragrance Of You

TO MY GIRLS WHO LIKE MY POETRY

I just had to really, stop and freeze,
As I smelled your fragrance, in the breeze.
I just could not, move my feet,
You smelled, so good and sweet.
The aroma absolutely, filled my nose,
You smelled like, a freshly cut rose.
My head got cloudy, and in a haze,
I was frozen there, and in a daze.
No other girl has ever, affected me this way.
I just couldn't think, of anything to say.
I just stood there, really dumbfounded,
Like a fast drum beat, my heart pounded.
I had to move quickly, to catch up to you,
So I could just walk, along side of you.
You're beauty, and your fragrance,
Has really made, quite a difference.
That's why I had, to stop and freeze,
As I smelled, your fragrance, in the breeze.

The One I've Been Looking For

Don't worry about, the sound you are hearing,
It's only my poor heart, that you're hearing.
It's not really, any kind of sweat,
It's from a lovely girl, I just met.
She just made my eyes, open up wide,
I just turned, to mush inside.
I was so captivated, at that time,
Out of my chest, my heart wanted to climb.
I couldn't think, of another thing,
She gave my heart, a hell of a ping.
I haven't felt this way, for quite awhile,
I just stood there, with a dumb ole smile.
I will tell you, I really am not dumb,
But, stick a fork in me, cause I am done.
My running around, was now done,
With her is where, I want to have all my fun.
I swear by the stars, moon and the sun,
I'll make our two hearts, beat as one.
"YOU ARE THE ONE, I'VE BEEN LOOKING FOR."

Thinking About You

If ever there would be, a girl for me,
You are the one, that it would be.
From all the other, girls I have seen,
I really want you, to be my queen.
We fit together like, the hand and glove,
I know it is you, that I truly love.
Your eyes sparkle, like an effervesent wine,
I want you to be with me, for all our time.
Your lips looks so, moist and sweet,
My lips to yours, just wants to meet.
Your hair has such, a beautiful, radiant glow
They are a few things, that make me love U so.
All I can do right now, is imagine your face,
And think about, a nice warm, loving embrace.
Do you think about, the same things about me?
And how our lives, could really be?
Time will really tell, how it will be,
All I know is that, I really love thee.

Very Unhappy

I'm as unhappy, as anyone can be,
Been looking for a girl, just for me.
As it was said, in the song,
It is true, in that song.
"Looking for love, in all the wrong places",
"Looking for love, in too many faces."
I have looked for love, almost everywhere,
All around from here, to way over there.
I am very tired, and about have given up,
Cause love hasn't even, ever shown up.
All I want is someone, to hold and love,
Someone to be here, and share all my love.
All I can offer you, is my love and me,
Can't you see how happy, that would make me?
You don't have to be, rich or famous,
Just share my love, between us.
"Looking for love, in all the wrong places,
Looking for love, in all the wrong faces."
This is why, "I am so unhappy."

When I Look At You

FOR A LOVE I HOPE TO FIND

When I stop, and look you,
Know what I see? When I look at you?
I see someone, with a certain flair,
A girl with long, and beautiful hair.
A girl who has, cool, baby blue eyes,
The same blue, we see, in our skies.
A figure that looks, like an hour glass,
I know she really, has some class.
Sometimes she looks, kind of out of place,
In some areas, with her beautiful face.
Her lips, they are so warm, soft and tender,
The most beautiful lips, I've seen, I remember.
And her fragrance, her aromatic smell.
Gives me a feeling, that I cannot quell.
You look like an angel, sent from up above,
I knew instantly, that I was in love.
You are my hopes, and my dreams come true,
I really want to be, only with you.
"I am so, In Love With You."

Whenever I See You

Whenever I see you, you give me a rush,
My poor heart, just turns to mush.
Whenever I see you, and your beautiful smile
I just gotta stop, and watch you awhile.
You really do some, strange things to me,
But it is hard to explain, what you to do me
Can't explain how, these things make me feel
All I know is, these feelings are real.
Whenever I see you, I get all shaky,
I feel the vibrations, take over me.
Whenever I see you, I can't think or speak,
And if I do, it just comes out as a squeek.
My heart went out, the first day I saw you,
All I can see, and think of, is only you.
Even from a distance, I've adored you,
I just really want, to be only with you.
Whenever I see you, you give me a rush,
And my poor heart, turns to mush.

You Are My Beautiful, Bright Shining Star

"TO MY SPECIAL LOVE"

Even tho I have to, love you from afar,
You are my beautiful, bright shining star.
And I see you shining, so very bright,
In the dark sky, each and every night.
I know it's you cause, I see you wink at me,
Just to make sure, it's you that I can see.
And it makes, my heart glow,
And it makes, me love you so.
You don't have to tell me, which way to go,
I'll follow your twinkling, wherever you go.
Coz even tho, I have to love you, from afar,
You are my beautiful, bright shining star.
Go anywhere and, I'll be there too,
Cause I am so, in love with you.
There's nowhere, you can go, without me,
I'll follow you, wherever, don't you see?
Coz even tho, I have to love you, from afar,
You are my beautiful, bright shining star.

You Have Brightened Up My Life

You have shown me, a brighter life,
Since you have, come into my life.
My life has been, dull and dreary,
And I have been, so darn weary.
But you have put, a little spark in my life,
A life that has been, full of daily strife.
Now all my thoughts, are all about you,
My mind is just, all about loving you.
I want us to live here, in my home,
So we don't have, to live all alone.
So bring, your loving heart, here with me,
We'll both be happier, being here with me.
Then we both can be, in each others arms,
And share our hearts, and loving charms.
I want to hold, caress, and love you,
Cause my darling, my heart, belongs to you.
One thing I want, in this life for me,
Is to be able to hold, kiss, and love thee.
This is how you have, Brightened Up My Life.

You Have Changed My Life

You led me to, such delights,
When you hold, me so tight.
I'm in heaven when, I am in your arms,
And you share with me, your lovely charms.
Tried to live without love, till I met you,
Now I know that, this is really not true.
Since we had our, very first slow dance,
I know I can't live, without your romance.
I am floating high, above the ground,
My tho'ts about love, has been turned around
You have changed my tho'ts, of love in a way
That's why I fell in love, with you that day.
Now I can't think, of anything but you,
Cause I am so much, in love with you.
With your beauty, and your sweet charms,
I just want to be, held in your arms.
I have never felt, this way before,
Of any girls that, I have known before.
"YOU HAVE CHANGED MY LIFE"

You Are Truly
My One Hearts Desire

You are truly, my one, hearts desire,
You have me sparking, like a live wire.
You have given me, a spark in my gizzards,
And it has lit up, all my innards.
It has really gotten hot, in my insides,
And it is a feeling, that I cannot hide.
When I look in the mirror, what do I see?
I see dancing hearts, for you from me.
And also flaming hearts, too that I see.
Cause you have, fired me up, don't you see?
You are truly, my one, heart's desire,
You have me sparking, like a live wire.
It's a feeling, that has died in me
You have rekindled, a new love for me.
Life now doesn't have to be, dark and dreary,
I got a new love now, thanks to you dearie.
You are truly, my one, heart's desire,
You got me sparking, like a live wire.

You Take My Breath Away

Every time you, walk my way,
Baby, you take, my breath away.
I feel kind of, lightheaded and hazy,
And this feeling has me, going a bit crazy.
You really don't know, what you do to me,
You are the only thing, or person that I see.
All I know is, when you come my way,
You really do, take my breath away.
You with your big, and beautiful smile,
I just have to stop, and watch you awhile.
You make my heart, do all kind of flip flops.
And it feels like it, just wants to stop.
I just want to wrap, my arms around you,
And kiss and hug you, the whole day through.
You make my insides, really go wild,
And this feeling is, far from being mild.
This is really why, I just have to say,
Baby, you really take, my breath away.

You're On Top

I just love, to hold you, in my arms,
And share all of, our loving charms.
You are so warm, soft, and lovely,
This is where, I always, want to be.
Your dreamy eyes, have put me in a spell,
They make, my poor heart, just swell.
The caress of your, soft loving touch,
Just makes me tingle, oh, so much.
And from your lips, your tender kiss,
Puts me into, a state, of wonderous bliss.
And I know there, are no demands,
As we walk, or stand, holding hands.
The feelings I have, that's just for you,
Are simple and true, and only for you.
My feelings and tho'ts, are these for sure,
And they are, wholesomely, very pure.
You have made my heart, go flippity flop,
On my most wanted list, "YOU'RE ON TOP".

My Daughters Birthday

September 24th, is Angel's birthday,
It's supposed to be, her special day.
I hope your every wish, does come true,
If anyone deserves it, it is you.
You try to be friends, with everyone,
Your heart is always, full of fun.
Angel is the name, you were given,
Cause your heart was sent, from heaven.
Yes, today is your birthday,
You deserve the best, in everyway.
You are my special, little one,
You are, second to none.
You've always been, my little Tinkerbell,
Cause you are, so very swell.
So, for you, my dear daughter,
I have been proud, to be your father.
So, on this very, special day,
Have a very, Happy Birthday.
I love you... Dad

My Four Daughters

THE LOVES OF MY LIFE, MY CHILDREN

I have four, lovely daughters,
One of my own, and three step-daughters.
I love them all, Equally,
With all my love, Unequivocally.
They are very, precious to me,
They are the greatest, can't you see?
For my, three step-daughters,
I do know, their real fathers.
But do not worry, everything is fine,
Cause all these years, they've been mine.
Here, a special song, has been sung,
We've been together, since they were young.
My real daughter is smart, and knows the score
She knows I love them all, all four.
I've loved them all, from the very start,
Each has a special place, in my heart.
I wouldn't trade them, for all the worldly gold,
Hark, Listen, Of this, you have been told.
"This is for, "My Four Daughters"

A Cowboy,
"My Time, In My Saddle"

The hot sun, is frying my brain,
As I sit in my saddle, looking over the range.
I watch the cattle, and keep them in line,
Trying to get them, to the market on time.
And keep them from, losing too much weight,
That means less money, and that's not great.
Like a woman, a cowboys work, is never done,
And we really don't have, a lot of real fun.
Driving a herd is really, long and hard,
This I mean to tell you, my friend and pard.
Once we're done, and back home again,
It's time to start, this all over again.
Whether it's winter, spring, summer or fall,
For these drives, we are always on call.
For families to survive, and make a living,
All our time, we have to, keep giving.
I get hand blisters, and saddle sores,
Once its done, it's time to do it, over again
A cowboy, ""MY TIME, IN MY SADDLE""

It's Almost Spring

Oh yes, it's almost spring,
Time for birds, to chirp and sing.
Soaring through the air, with the greatest of ease,
Flappin' and sailing, in the warm spring breeze.
On yes, it's almost spring,
Even people walk, and hum, and sing,
Crickets will start, to chirp loud and clear,
For all of us, to listen and hear.
Time for lovers to court, and fall in love,
Knowing they were sent together, from up above.
It's been such, a long, long year,
For spring to come around again, this year.
Oh yes, it's almost spring!

Hugs

FOR A WORLD OF LOVE AND HUGS

My heart is, full of hugs,
And my heart, you do tug.
I will open, my arms real wide,
So that you can, step inside.
I will give you, a great big hug,
All you have to do, is return that hug.
It won't cost you, hardly anything, you see,
A little energy, to return that hug to me.
This world needs more, love and hugs,
Go get someone else, and give them a hug.
If we all find someone, to give a hug,
Then they will find, someone else to hug.
And if we all find, someone to hug,
This world will be, a love place for hugs.
So grab someone, and give them a hug,
You'll be glad, you gave 'em a hug.

My New Found Friend

Gina, the name, of my new found friend,
She's a friend, with whom I can contend
She is very sweet, and very witty,
And as frisky, as a little kitty.
She has, my curiousity, going wild,
And pretty giddy, as a small child.
Out of her head, funny things just pop,
To me she is, the cream of the crop.
She makes me laff, and feel good inside,
I rock and roll, just like the tide.
Haven't felt like this, in quite awhile
A message from her, just makes me smile
Gina you are so, kind and sweet,
To me you are, a very nice treat.
I hope we can continue, to be friends,
Cause you never know, how it will end.
Something else, I wouldn't think twice
To become closer, would be very nice.

Stars, Night and Love

The stars are shining, big and bright,
On this clear, and beautiful night.
Everything seems to be, just so right,
In each others arms, sharing their delight.
No one could come, between these two,
Nothing else matters, to these two.
Caught up in each others, sweet embrace,
Their minds completely, in outer space.
Sweet and slow, they share their love,
Which was sent to them, from up above.
Their love couldn't, be for any other,
These two were meant, just for each other.
Locked in an embrace, of eternal bliss,
That is for this guy, and his miss.
They fit together, like a hand and glove,
That is how much, these two, are in love.

The Coming Of Dawn

After this long, cold, winters night,
The sun comes up, big and bright.
Tis, "The Coming Of Dawn."
As I wait, with much delight,
For the suns, morning light.
Tis, "The Coming Of Dawn."
Oh My! Such a beautiful sight!
To see the sun rise, big and bright.
Tis, "The Coming Of Dawn."
I wonder if anyone else, feels this way,
Waiting for the beginning, of a brand new day.
Tis, "The Coming Of Dawn."
As I sit watching, upon this hill,
Seeing the sunrise, gives me such a thrill.
Cause it is, "The Coming Of Dawn."

Why Do I Love Poetry?

Why do I love poetry?
Because it soothes the hearts, of you, and me.
It can be written, about many things,
Even about someone's, friendship ring.
Pets, scenes, or our every day lives,
About loving husbands, and their wives.
You think, and write, about any theme,
You make a reader's eyes, "surely gleam."
Why do I love poetry?
Cause it shows personal feelings, about you, and me.
Poetry, is something given, "absolutely free,"
To warm the hearts, of you, and me.
Surely about warm, sweet, tender love,
For all the reasons, I've listed above.
This is the reason, I love poetry!